VAL**END**TINE

_hydrus

Copyright © 2022 Hydrus
Cover Copyright © 2022 Hydrus

All rights reserved.

The characters depicted in this book are fictitious. Any similarity to real persons, living or dead, is coincidental and not intended by the author.

The scanning, uploading, and distribution of this book without permission is a theft of the author's intellectual property. If you would like permission to use material from the book (other than for review purposes), please contact hydruspoetry@gmail.com. Thank you for your support of the author's rights.

Published by: Hydrus
Photography & Illustrated Art by: Hydrus
Cover Design by: Cleo Moran - Devoted Pages Designs
Formatting by: Cleo Moran - Devoted Pages Designs
https://www.devotedpages.com
Proofreading: Amina Jojo Dahmouche

Manufactured in the United States of America

The Library of Congress Cataloging-in-Publication Data is available upon request.

Paperback ISBN: 979-8-9856109-0-1
E-Book ISBN: 979-8-9856109-1-8

hydrus

Dedicated to All of Us
who play in the Dark

ValENDtine

My latest collection of poems is comprised of some of lifes most steamy, sensual, and erotic situations. It tackles feelings of desire and dark passion through the lens of love and lust.

The poems take us through this journey. Letting our minds and hearts wander throughout this lustful escape. Searching and yearning at each and every turn for a new encounter or blushing moment…. maybe a few hot and bothered ones as well.

All the poems in ValENDtine can be found throughout all my prior collections including some from my online postings.

In addition to these poems, I also have written several new ones that are exclusive only to the ValENDtine collection.

I hope you enjoy the poems as much as I enjoyed writing them. May this new collection find a permanent place on your nightstand.

Live to Love
_hydrus

Let me drown in

what I cannot have

hydrus

Only her hands
Belonged on me
It knew my strengths
And every need

It rubbed my skin
And felt my chest
Gripped my arms
Muscles and pecs

Rode my bones
Wrapped her legs
Squeezed the moans
That made us beg

Took me in
To coat my spill
Inside every core
We ravaged our will

Owned
_hydrus

Hidden eyes
Spying forms
Pleasured beats
Bounded norms

Masters rules
Obeying hands
Lucid grips
Spanked commands

Restrained hunger
Arousing scent
Judges sentence
No repent

Knotted wrists
Leathers worn
Open mouths
Clothes are torn

Hands and knees
A prepped display
Behaved attraction
Ready to play

Waiting
_hydrus

Tender lips are gliding
Arched neck placed in hand
Feeling slowly finding
Listening to commands

Wanting just to ravage
Buried in drenched lust
Tamed you have the savage
Moans at every thrust

In Charge
_hydrus

Threaded limbs
Enter every curve
Soft embraces
Waken every nerve

Sleep still lingers
Anxious hands explore
Dormant flesh
Waiting for some more

Sliding kisses
Move to take their mark
Entering spaces
To ignite a spark

Once they meet
Gentle licks will glide
Tasting heat
So deep inside

Yearning
_hydrus

MY HERO
BE MINE
SUGAR PIE
YOUDA BEST
U GOT THIS
YOU + ME
SUPER STAR
GO 4 IT
HONEY BUN
LOVE BUG
U GOT THIS

Ride what you own
Etch what you took
— hydrus

Fingers trace
Every moan
Body clenched
Sweaty groans

Tender lips
Soft caress
Panting kiss
Beaded breasts

Lavish scent
Drained of sin
Warm licks
On tender skin

Whispered treats
On bedded silk
Hardened veins
Quenched in milk

Wrapping legs
Mounting bones
Selfish acts
All alone

Divine
_hydrus

Light the candles
Dim the lights
Pull back the sheets
For the night

Lay down slowly
On your side
Feel my hands
Gently glide

Close your eyes
Lick your lips
Daddys searching
For a sip

Give him what
He came to drink
Between your hips
Tasting your pink

Bliss
_hydrus

Lets always Begin by Pinching, Twisting Biting and Sucking

hydrus

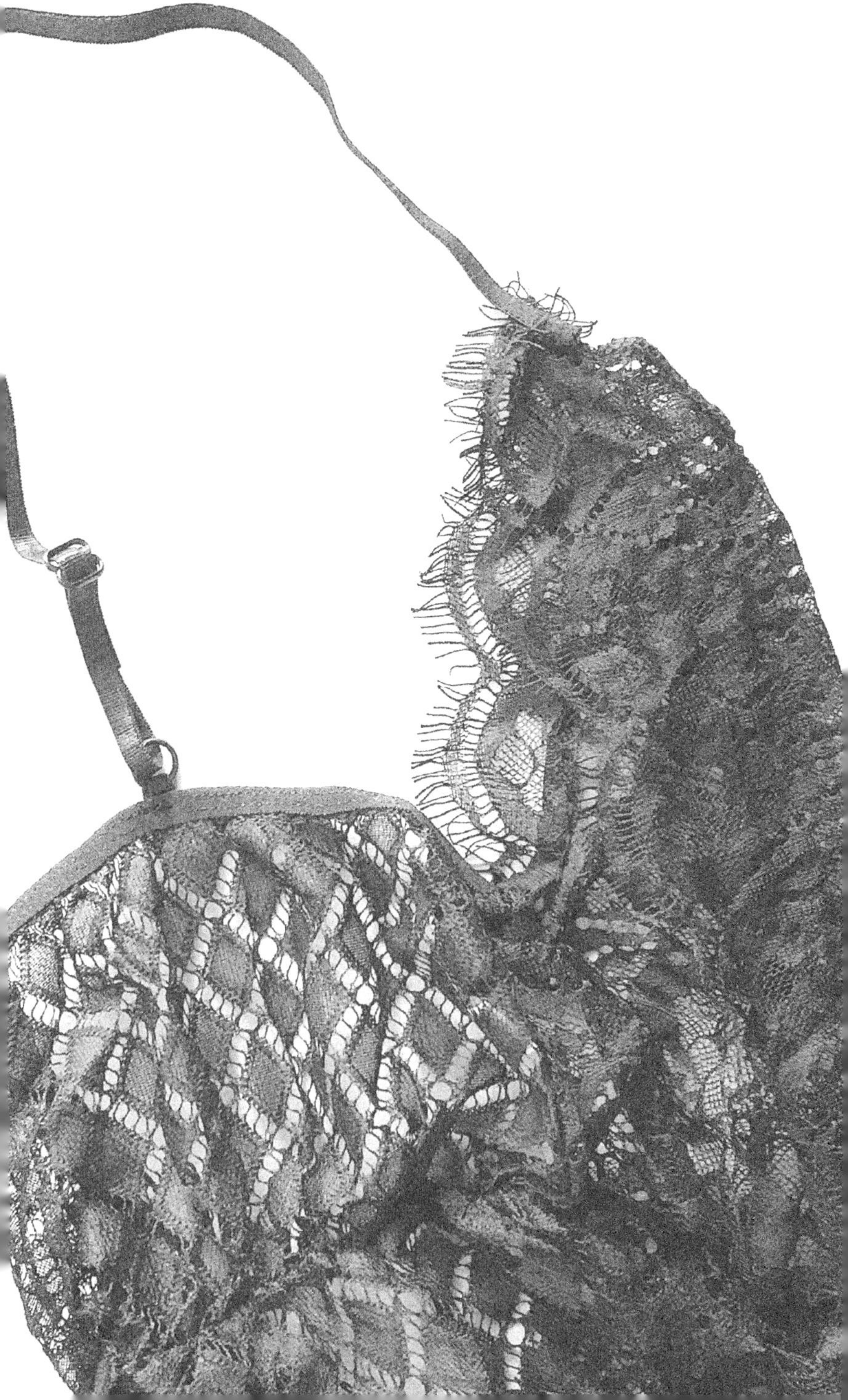

Edging every inch
Into spilling raging storms
The tides were fiercely wild
Her fingers savagely worn

Waiting to consume
His thick and hardened girth
Throbbing every vein
Showing her his worth

Spreading for the mount
Pushing into claim
His member quickly filled
Starvation was to blame

Now she felt him whole
Her needs were at ease
Craving for this chance
Temptations crave to please

Patience
_hydrus

Feel your friction
As you grind
Take whats yours
Dont be kind

Leave your marks
I will fill your holes
Take whats mine
So you lose control

Prop
_hydrus

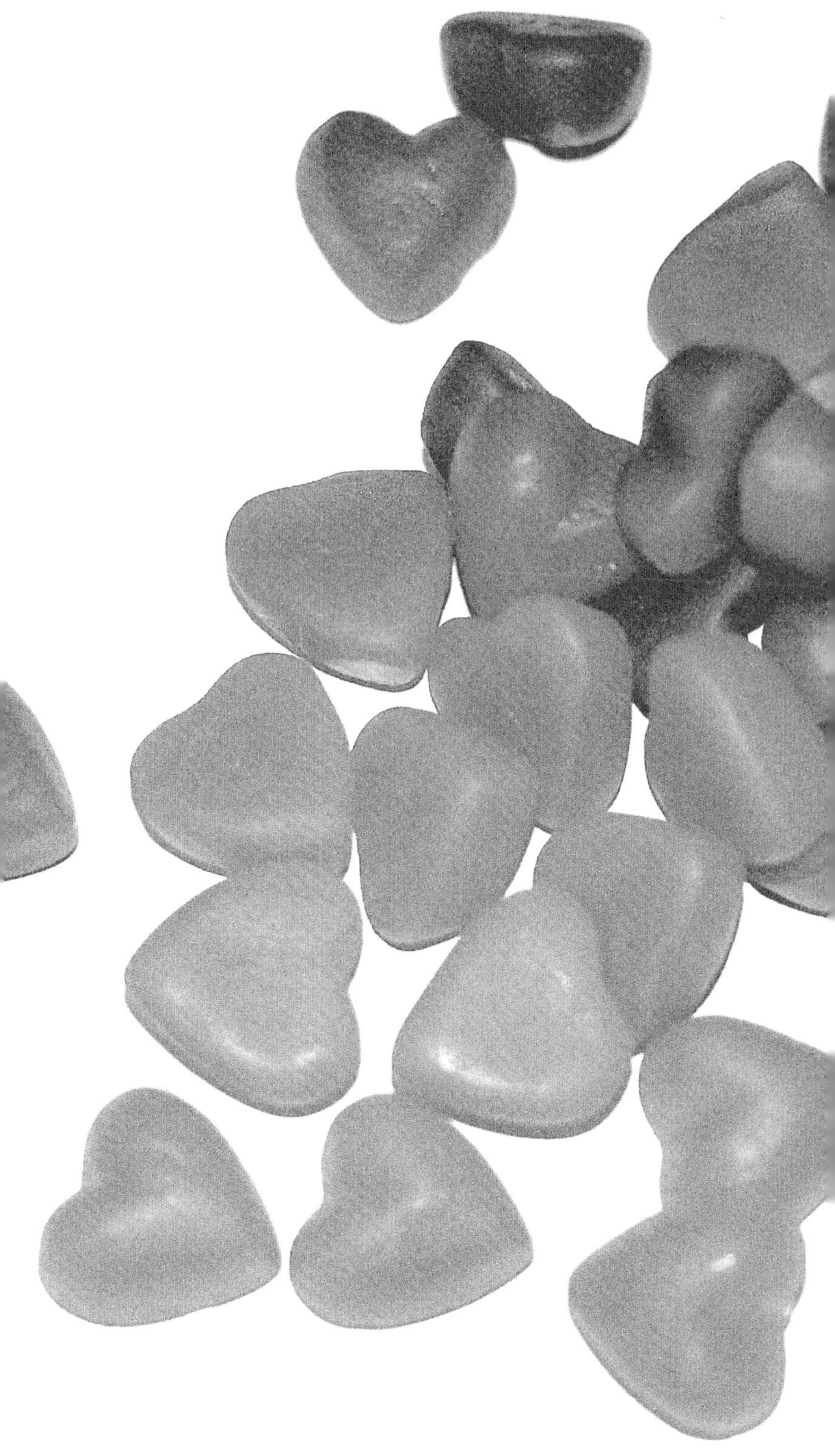

Devour every scent
That you create

-hydrus

I feel you dripping
Down your thighs
My hands are wet
Look in my eyes

Feel my fingers
Take your waves
Lick them each
To misbehave

Feed them to you
Taste your bliss
Give it back
In every kiss

Let our hunger
Never cease
Drink each other
As we release

Flavor
_hydrus

Take the ropes
From my hands
Tie yourself
Where you stand

Ill make the knots
Squeeze them tight
Bend you over
For my delight

Let my tongue
Search your skin
Every place
Every sin

Beg with moans
Mouth is drenched
Ache for this
As you clench

Begging
_hydrus

Take a seat
Where I will dine
Upon my mouth
So I can take my time

Grind and push
As I rub and taste
Every drop
That you let escape

Meal
_hydrus

Outstretched wandering hands
Devouring embrace
Gorging on wet lips
Drunken sensuous state

Wicked captive stare
Yearning for a taste
Nails ripping to tear
Holding you in haste

Hostage in your arms
Tongue starts to trace
Feasting on your throat
Mouth finds its place

Bitten
_hydrus

Leave your scent
In every space
Let it drip
Onto my face

Take your taste
From my lips
Eat everything
That is our bliss

Painted
_hydrus

Clench your hands
And watch me bend
Grip whats yours
No more pretend

Pull and tug
As I grow
Stroke my length
Until you blow

Down
_hydrus

Let your fin

rs find me

hydrus

Mangled hair
Bed sheets thrown
Pillows hide
Shredded gown

Lip red blush
Pounding flesh
Bodies crushed
Moaning hushed

Wetness sweat
Feelings kept
Desire felt
As I knelt

Taken
_hydrus

Awakened senses
Lips lightly breach
Snatching moans
Pulsating peach

Gently stroked
Welcoming warmth
Ravaged play
Toying roles

Muscles clench
Bitten skin
Morning bliss
You within

Swollen
_hydrus

Let me eat all your petals
As I drip upon your thorns
Open up your garden
Take a seat upon my horns

Ravage
_hydrus

Feel my lips
As they go inside
Taking you
For a blissful ride

Quench our thirst
As you open up
Let me drink
To fill up my cup

Take your legs
Tie us in a knot
Grind my face
As you hit your spot

All of me
Is in all of you
Never stop
Theres so much to do

Play
_hydrus

Trace what y

made me do

-hydrus

Slip into
Something red
I need to eat
To be fed

Let the lace
Show every curve
The ones I lick
Lap every nerve

Bring that body
That I thirst
Wildly drink
Your every burst

Take me in
As I beg
Push down my head
Between your legs

I will taste
All your bliss
Tongue deep inside
With every kiss

Slowly trace
Push me in
Until you come
So I begin

Prologue
_hydrus

Binging on your beauty
Thirsting for a taste
Dripping from arousal
Licking every space

How I yearn to drink you
Devouring every sip
Savoring this moment
Lapping luscious lips

Parched
_hydrus

Take a seat
Put your hands behind
Let me dance
And watch me grind

Ride your crotch
As I feel you swell
Fill your veins
Your looks will tell

Grab my hips
Look in my eyes
Rub this skin
Go up my thighs

Take your hands
And coat them well
Watch you throb
Grow and swell

Bounce some more
See you jerk
Make you hard
Twerk and work

Beg and moan
To make you come
In control
Your time is done

Pro
_hydrus

Hair draped skin
Softly soaked
Droplets streaking
Movements evoke

Sensuous lines
Smoothly arouse
Desired stroking
Suggestive browse

Alluring stares
Enticing grins
Fingers calling
Heat within

Quiet intention
Hands roam
Passionate tension
Primal moans

Drenched
_hydrus

Tie me up the way

want to be tied

hydrus

Roll right over
And find your way
I have been waiting
All night and day

Let me ease
Your every care
Close your eyes
Lets disappear

In this moment
Theres only us
Feel my hands
I slowly thrust

Feeling your darkness
My soul arrives
Inside your spirit
I come alive

Always One
_hydrus

Close your eyes and let my tongue be your escape

—hydrus

Dark lit room
Engulfs our shapes
Tender kisses
Slowly trace

Wondering eyes
Captured trance
Hidden pleasures
Starved romance

Escape we must
Lies to place
Our hearts we trust
Leave no trace

A life together
Fates our plan
Lets disappear
To start again

Runaway
_hydrus

Under the blankets
Begging to receive
Undressed with my illusions
Solely yearning to appease
Forbidden to escape
Lured and tied to please
Throbbing to taste
Grinding to such ease
Filling our thirst
Holding to what is mine
Heated in my bursts
All we have is time

Infinite
_hydrus

Gentle lips caress my neck
Slowly they persist to taste
Our mouths begin to inspect
Hands wander to trace

Stares and sighs exchange
Our bodies quickly tighten
Dampened flesh engages
Internal voices fighting

Devoured skin is breached
A moment held in time
All sorrows are released
Now conquered you are mine

Property
_hydrus

Tell me more
About your dreams
Every desire
Every scream

What positions
Did we play
Did I hunt you
As my prey

Were you captured
By your beast
Spread wide open
For his feast

Did he eat you
Till you came
Woken up
By your rains

Awake
_hydrus

You are the passion

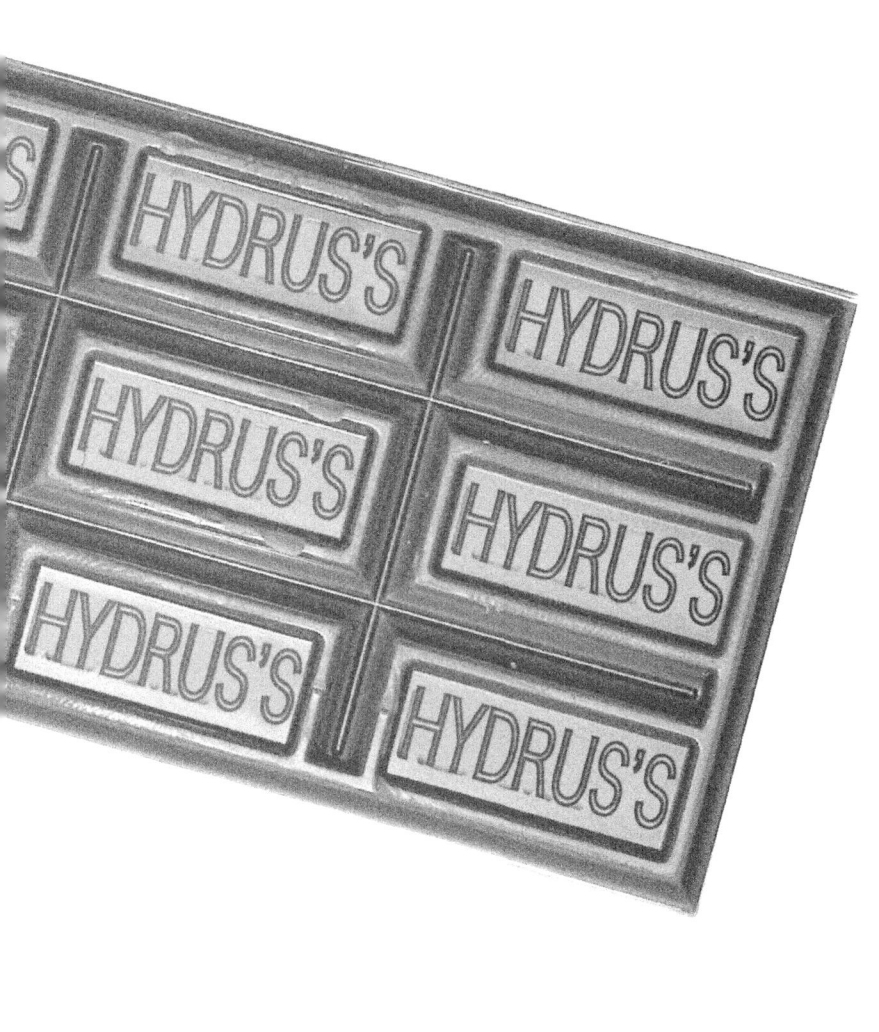

always want to fill

hydrus

Her skin tender
Lightly iced
In my arms
Warmth ignites

Soft kisses
And bitten lips
Tasting tongues
With fingertips

Pounding hearts
Tracing lines
Indulging movements
Bodies grind

Tingling feelings
Breathless air
This forever
No compare

Endless
_hydrus

Run your nails
Down my back
Dig them in
As we snack

Lift you up
As I go deep
Wrap your legs
Hook your feet

Find a wall
Where you will rest
Brace yourself
Pounding flesh

Heavy breathing
Shaking moans
Pushing hard
Stretching groans

Feel you drip
Coat your man
Endless pleasures
Where we stand

Pressed
_hydrus

Lost in your words
Painted mazes
Smoke filled rooms
Sexy phrases

Undressed thoughts
Closing eyes
Wanting you
Butterflies

Lips on skin
Passions brew
Hunger stings
Is it true

Delusion
_hydrus

Distant lips
They burn to taste
Soft and wet
Begging to trace

Let them feel
Sipping desire
Quenching thirst
Putting out their fire

Pour
_hydrus

I want to disappear
Where only you can feel me

—hydrus

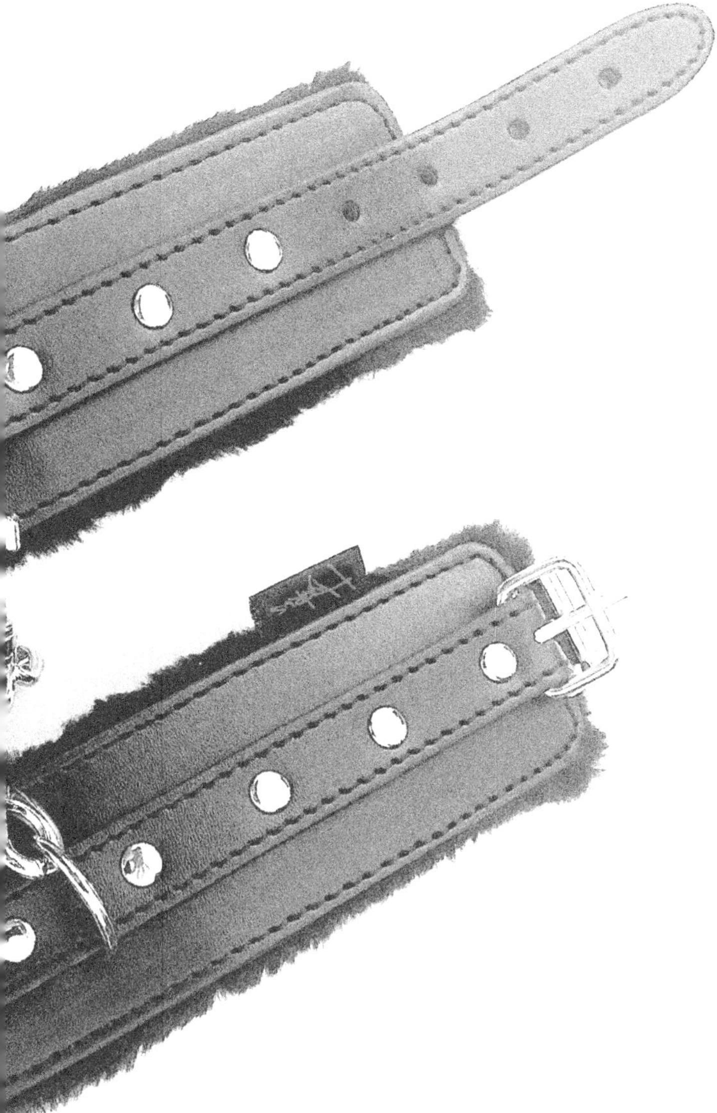

In the dark
Between our sheets
I slowly devour
Whats for me

Selfish cravings
As petals spread
Feeling her hands
Pushing my head

Dawn
_hydrus

Let me pinch your peach
Rub it with my thumb
Leave yourself wide open
Watch you slowly come

Let me take myself
Playing with your lips
Gripping what is yours
Pressing on my tip

Coating all your fingers
Driving them so deep
Let me hear your bliss
Dripping as I seep

Immersed
_hydrus

I want to be the first kiss you taste and the last kiss you drink

—hyphens

Black lips
Find my skin
A tender kiss
Love within

Fingertips
Caress my brow
Hands on hips
In the now

Neck back
Throat exposed
No more mask
No more clothes

Nails scratch
Streak and tear
Exposed skin
So unaware

Passions rough
Lust divine
Captured trust
Forever mine

Darken Hall
_hydrus

Hands upon my chest
Slowly moving down
Reaching and feeling
Gripping what is found

Pulling on my girth
Veins throbbing in hand
Pulsing feeling warm
Waiting for commands

The Arousal
_hydrus

Wandering stare
Words caress
Yearning skin
Morning undress

Figure in water
Outlined in mist
Wishful desires
Stolen glimpse

Drop painted flesh
Fingers will chase
Tempestuous form
Lips will retrace

Rendezvous
_hydrus

Eyes on me
Spread your legs
Arch your back
Want you to beg

Feel my hands
On your throat
Sliding in
Clench to coat

Take you rough
Where we stand
Ravage flesh
To my demands

Fill you up
Fuel your fire
Sore and wet
With my desire

Erupt
_hydrus

Every vein drips for you

hydrus

Used for desire
Pride of all scent
Cannot be captured
Guilty lament

Whispers of leather
Moans in the dark
One so clever
Whips make their mark

Grunting silence
Shadows dress flesh
Abundant desires
A slippery sketch

Taste on a finger
Hunger endures
Mounted upon us
Stained tiled floors

Ravish and conjure
A thirst to be quenched
Skin upon skin
Oiled and drenched

Motionless lines
Shattered doors opened wide
Soul has been taken
Nothing to hide

Hidden Pleasures
_hydrus

Midnight lifts
As neon blinks
Smokey mist paints
Ink filled wrists

Stares of lust
Lace whiskey sips
Tongues that lap
Thirst for drips

Moments pass
Hands reach their mark
Tracing lines
Plunge in the dark

Muscles tense
A strangers kiss
Seductive secrets
Uncover bliss

Motive
_hydrus

Sitting in darkness
I stare at the flicker
Of a wanted moan
A thirst grows thicker

Melting hot wax
Slowly drips to unveil
A hardened thick shaft
You kneel without fail

Gripping my skin
As you lick to oblige
Our trance reconnects
I look in your eyes

Take what is yours
Devour me whole
I am yours to command
You are mine to control

One
_hydrus

Lets make our darkest

secrets come true

hydrus

Arch your back
Open wide
Let me see
Where I will slide

Breathless moan
Clenching gape
I must consume
Eat every shape

Push me in
Mark my face
As I lick
Every trace

Lets devour
As we pinch
Take me whole
Every inch

Breakfast
_hydrus

Luscious Lips
Dripping red
Drenching tip
Painted head
Licking shaft
Throbbing veins
Every muscle
Gently played
Bodies bend
Stroking skin
Whispered groans
Sensual grins
Open throat
Takes me in
Ingested moans
Morning sin

Sunrise
_hydrus

Sit and stare
Watch me play
Take whats yours
Misbehave

Do the same
We both watch
Each other take
What we cannot

Dip your fingers
As I stroke
Rub your lips
I slowly choke

Lets both come
Feel our waves
Both deep inside
Explode and play

Witness
_hydrus

Take your hands
Unzip your dress
Crawl to me
I must confess

On your knees
Pull me out
Lick your lips
Tongue is out

Place me deep
As I push in
Feel your throat
Drink my sin

Look at me
You are not done
Swallow all
We just begun

Date
_hydrus

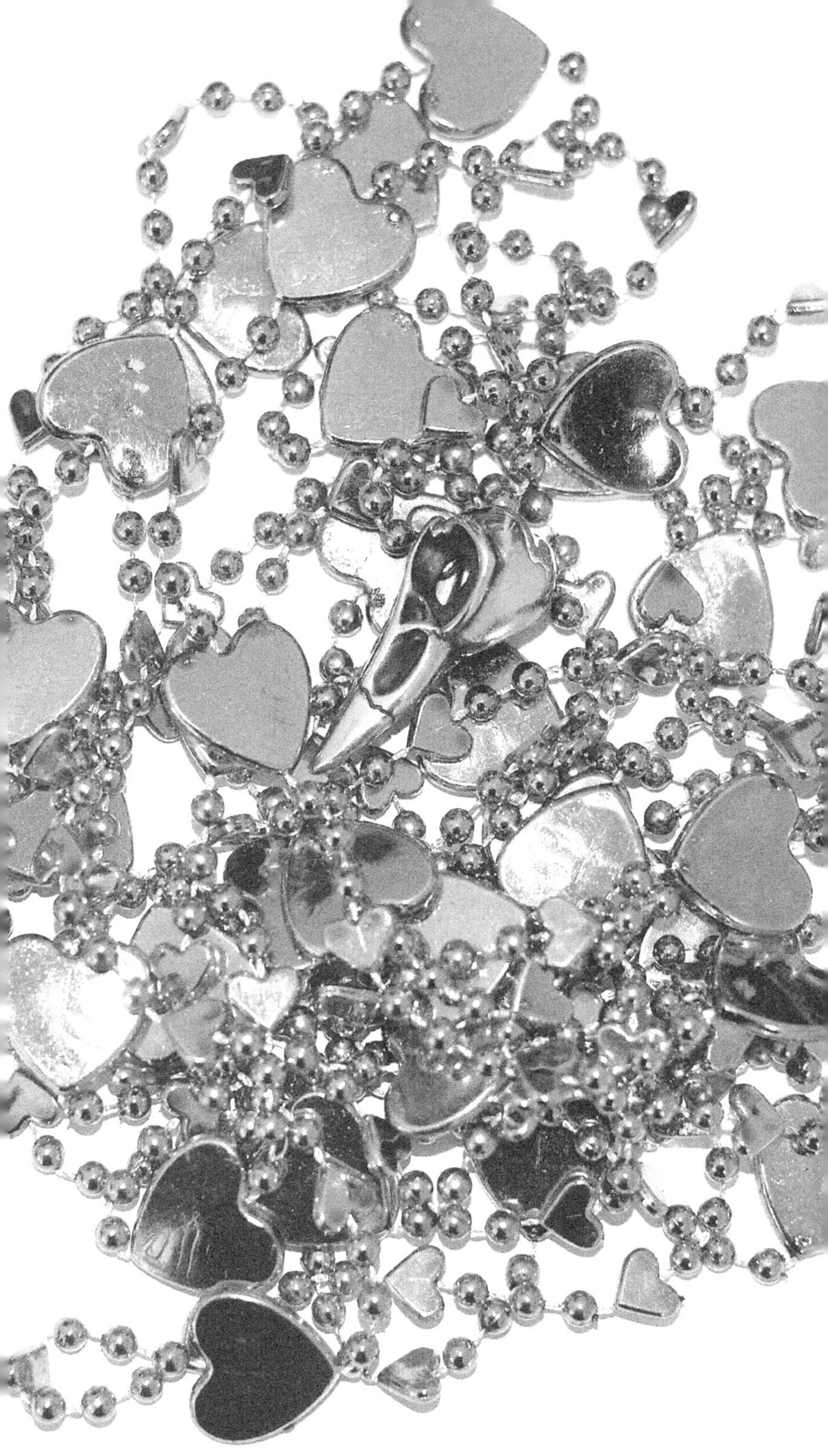

You Live on My fingers

hydrus

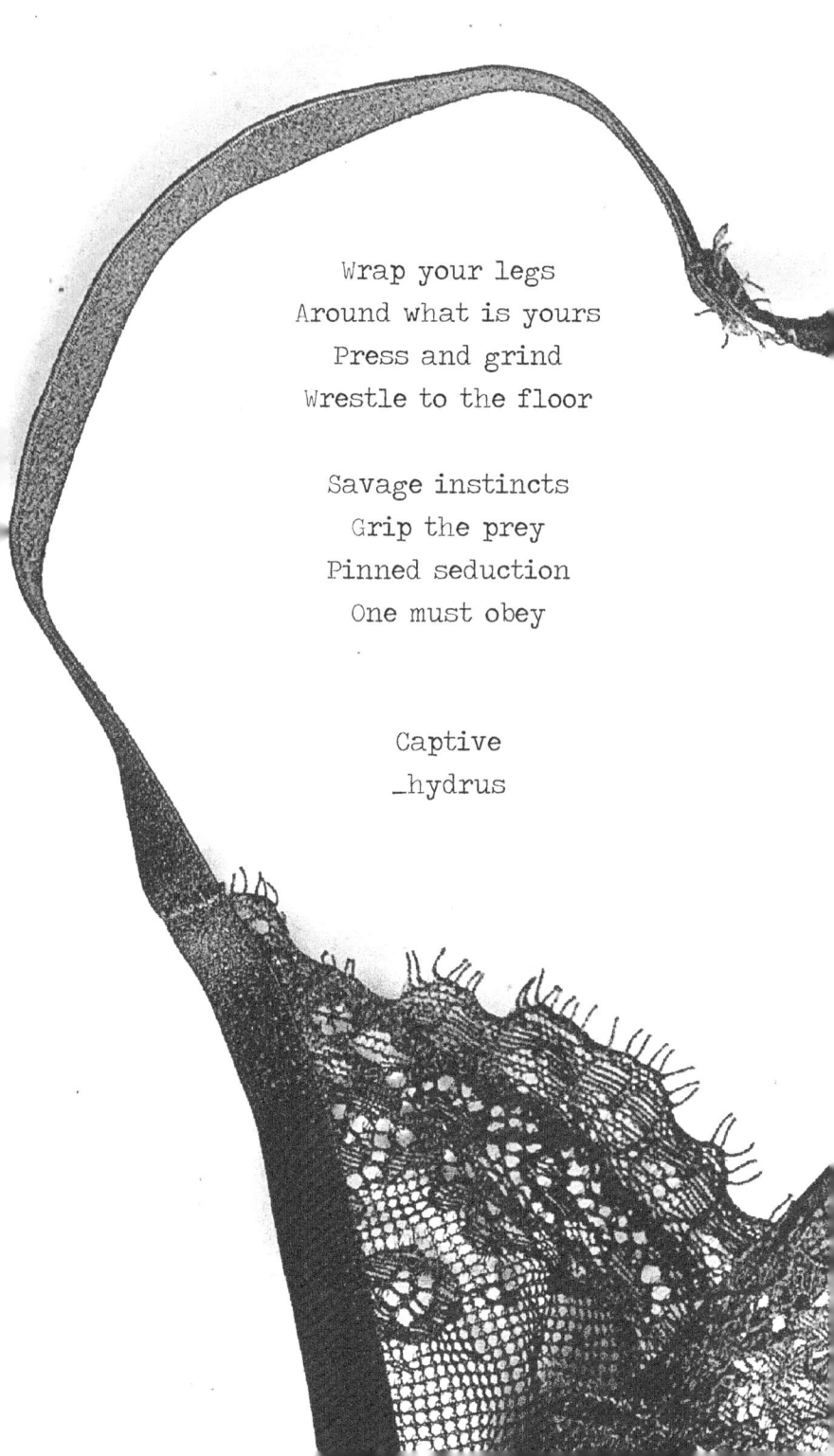

Wrap your legs
Around what is yours
Press and grind
Wrestle to the floor

Savage instincts
Grip the prey
Pinned seduction
One must obey

Captive
_hydrus

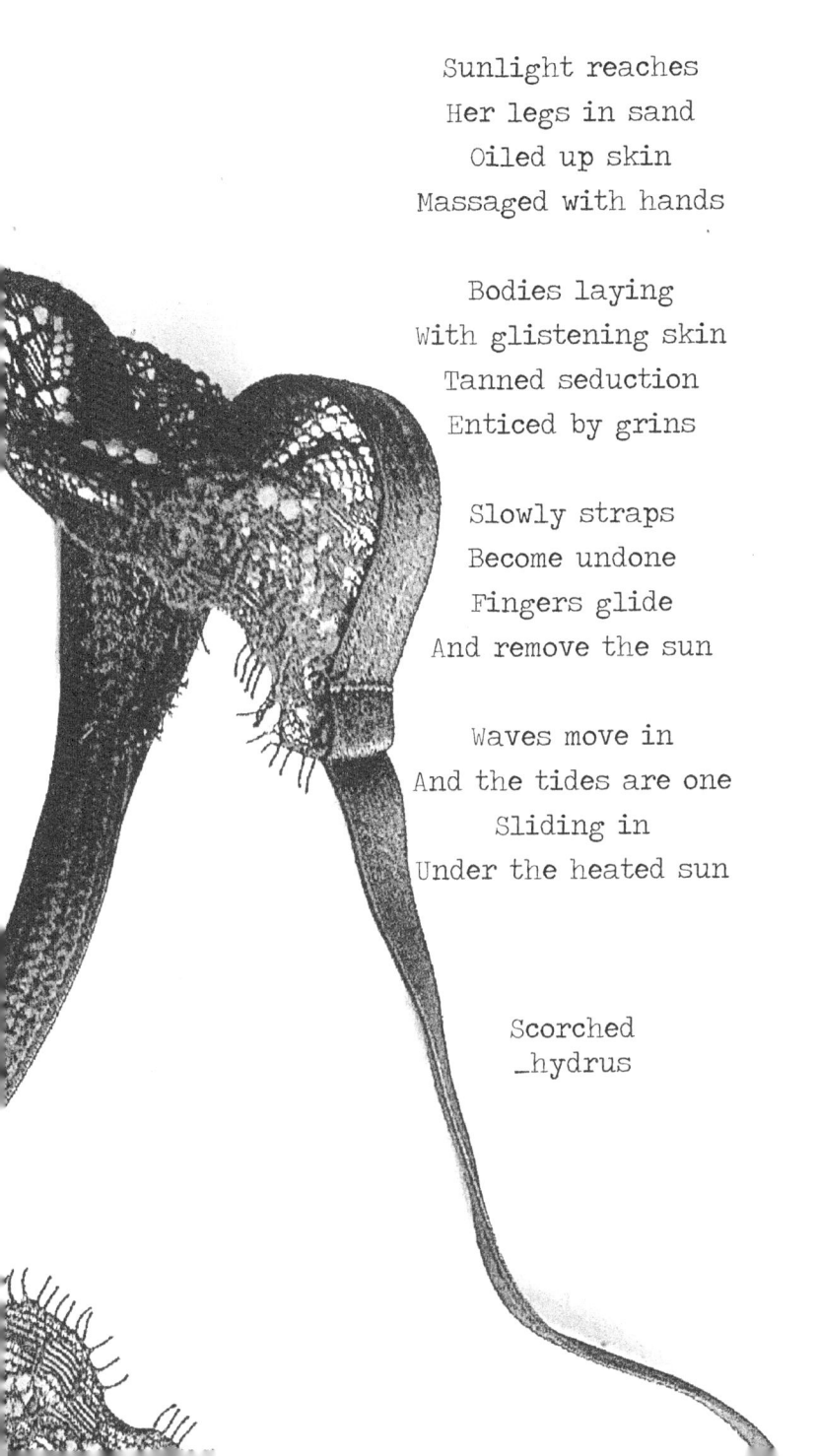

Sunlight reaches
Her legs in sand
Oiled up skin
Massaged with hands

Bodies laying
With glistening skin
Tanned seduction
Enticed by grins

Slowly straps
Become undone
Fingers glide
And remove the sun

Waves move in
And the tides are one
Sliding in
Under the heated sun

Scorched
_hydrus

Hush be silent
Let no one see
Get on your knees
Let me feed you please

Everyone around us
Have no clue
The things we hunger
The things we do

Slide me in
Or take my hand
Crouched or standing
Listen to commands

Both bodies moan
As their scents desire
Fill all needs
To quench their fires

Public
_hydrus

Candles glowing
Petals placed
Scented air
Yearning taste

Spread flesh
Angled form
Wetness drips
Clothes are torn

Hands on girth
Sensuous lips
Fingers pry
Inserted tip

Deep inside
Prints on skin
Passion rides
Forbidden sin

Wanting
_hydrus

Clean up our mess b

e we make it again

-hydrus

Fingerprints
Adorn my thighs
Where her hands
Found their prize
Inner walls
Lapped to ease
Arching backs
As lovers please
Intertwined
Bodies twist
Drenched in oils
Lips are kissed
Tongues explore
Inside we dive
Soaked in lust
Feeling so alive

Encounter
_hydrus

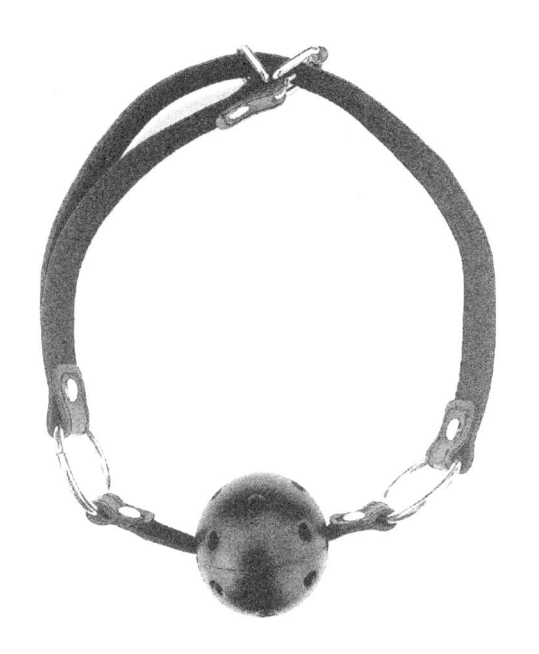

Let my lips hold
Your every whisper
And return it
As a moan

hydrus

Invisible the cages
Trapped in our skin
Craving such rages
Bursting with sin

Hungering to take you
Ravaging the soul
Failing to resist us
Devouring you whole

Sipping every inch
Drowning in your flesh
Spreading as I pinch
Bodies breathlessly mesh

Drenched in pure passion
Heated in embrace
Inside one another
Leaving my trace

The List
_hydrus

Sun bathes her body
Waves embracing shapes
Slowly fingers searching
Longing for escape

Ripples dance on waves
Sand caressing skin
Washing sins in sight
Burying cravings within

Carnal winds arouse
Constantly yearning to take
Our flame never burns out
Destiny found us too late

Stranded
_hydrus

On this table
We always ate
With our mouths
Without plates

Here the wood
Marks your spot
Hungry hands
Tied their knots

Drenched in oil
Cut the knives
Dipped the spoon
Looked in your eyes

We served each other
On this bed
Inside forever
We always fed

Full
_hydrus

Tie me up... I want to beg

hydrus

Put your hands on my

at... where they belong

Gentle the kisses
That traced down my neck
Slowly they ventured
Explored to inspect

Every inch tasted
Muscles contract
Nothing resisted
Just our first act

Mission
_hydrus

Laying in bed
Wishing you were here
Under the covers
Touching all to feel

My hands resting
Upon your back
Gently massaging
Ready to attack

Thirsting to drink you
Pull your hair
Mark your body
Eat you rare

How I yearn
For your return
Laying in wait
As my body burns

Arrival
_hydrus

Longing for your body
Savagely intense
Anxious to devour
Slow is the descent

Craving my obsession
Viciously I feast
Drenched in raw emotion
Moaning is the beast

Claimed
_hydrus

Under your sheets
My fingers beg
Slow is their search
Upon your legs

They famishedly trace
A scent is reached
Hands are placed
They found their peace

Lured
_hydrus

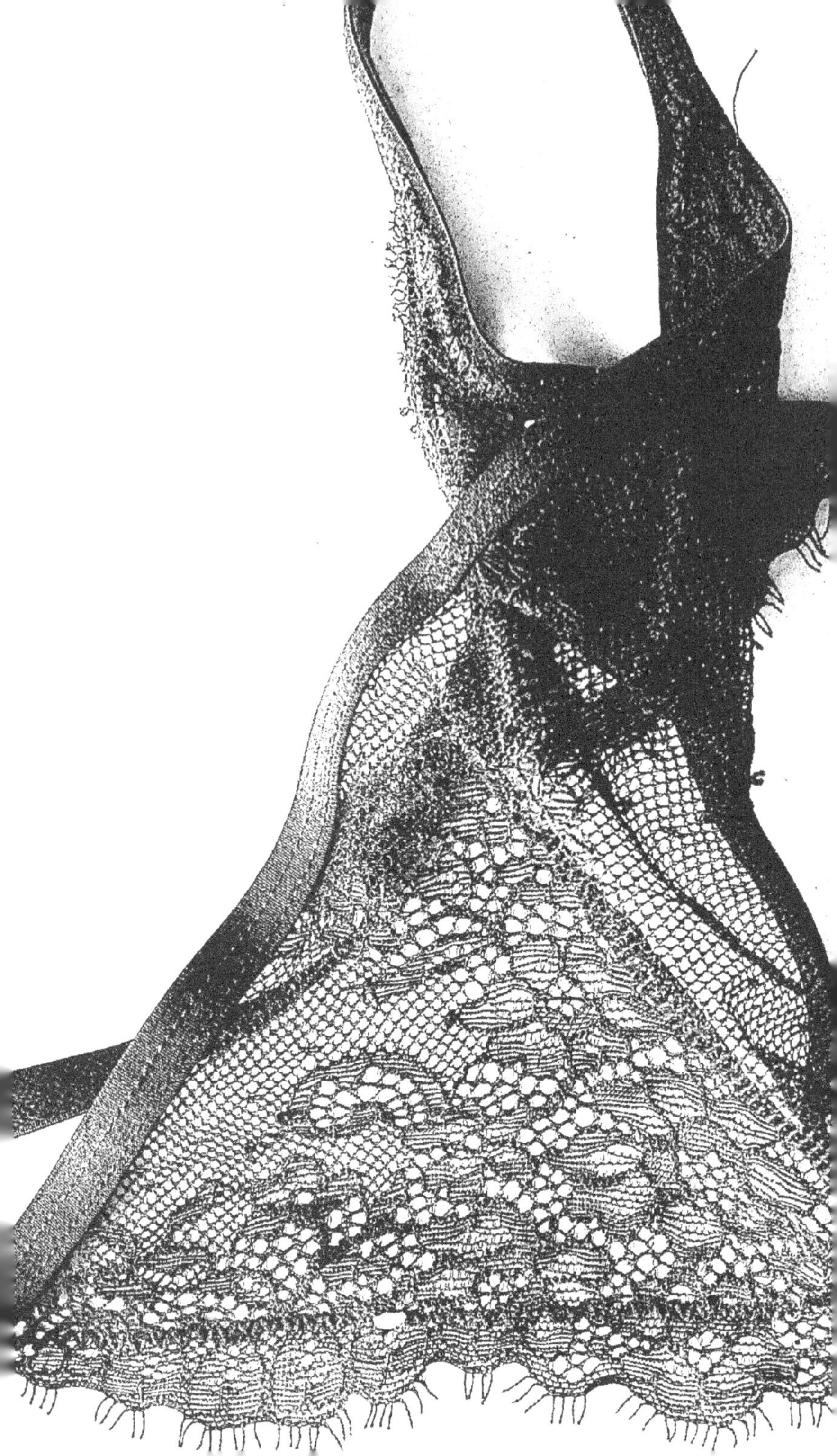

Bury my hands
Where the world cant see
How much pleasure
Rains beneath

I want to drink
Everything you give
All your bliss
Is where I live

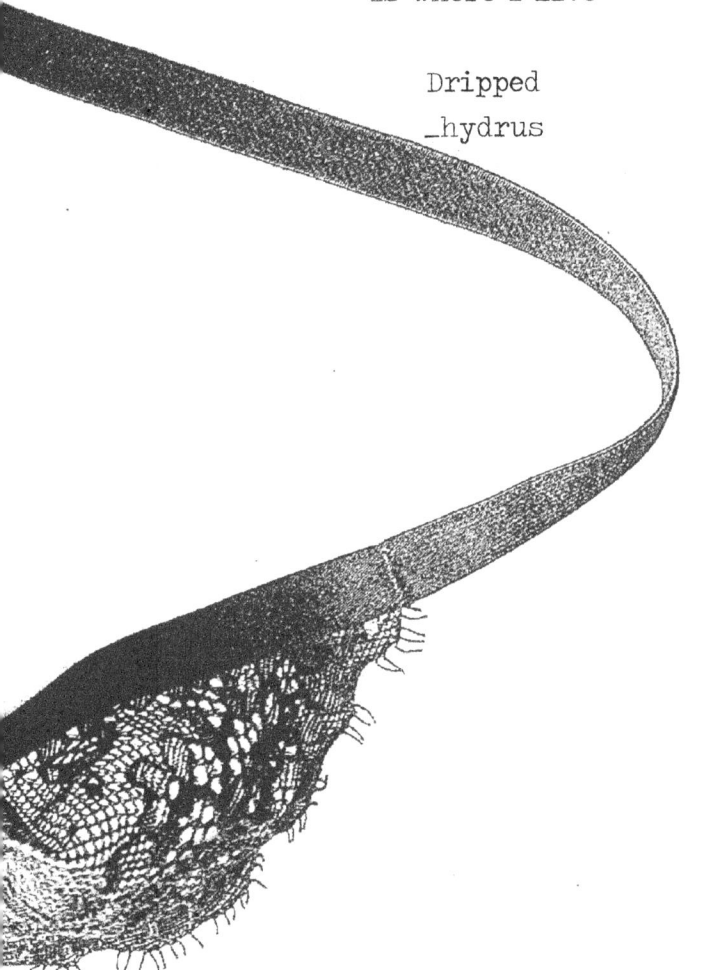

Dripped
_hydrus

Morning light settles
Sheets begin to peel
Eyes begin to hunt
Hands grabbing to feel

Devoured by flesh
Craving my descent
Buried in passion
Tasting all your scent

Legs quickly wrapping
Anchor to my skin
Pulling bodies close
Lunging into sin

Hunger
_hydrus

Savage steps
Attract a look
Yearning lips
On the hook

Tempted fate
Drew her in
Hunger came
Hard within

Fingers grab
Pull in close
Flesh aroused
Take in host

Pounding skin
Beating heart
Grinding bones
Naked art

Temptress
_hydrus

Spank Me with your Words

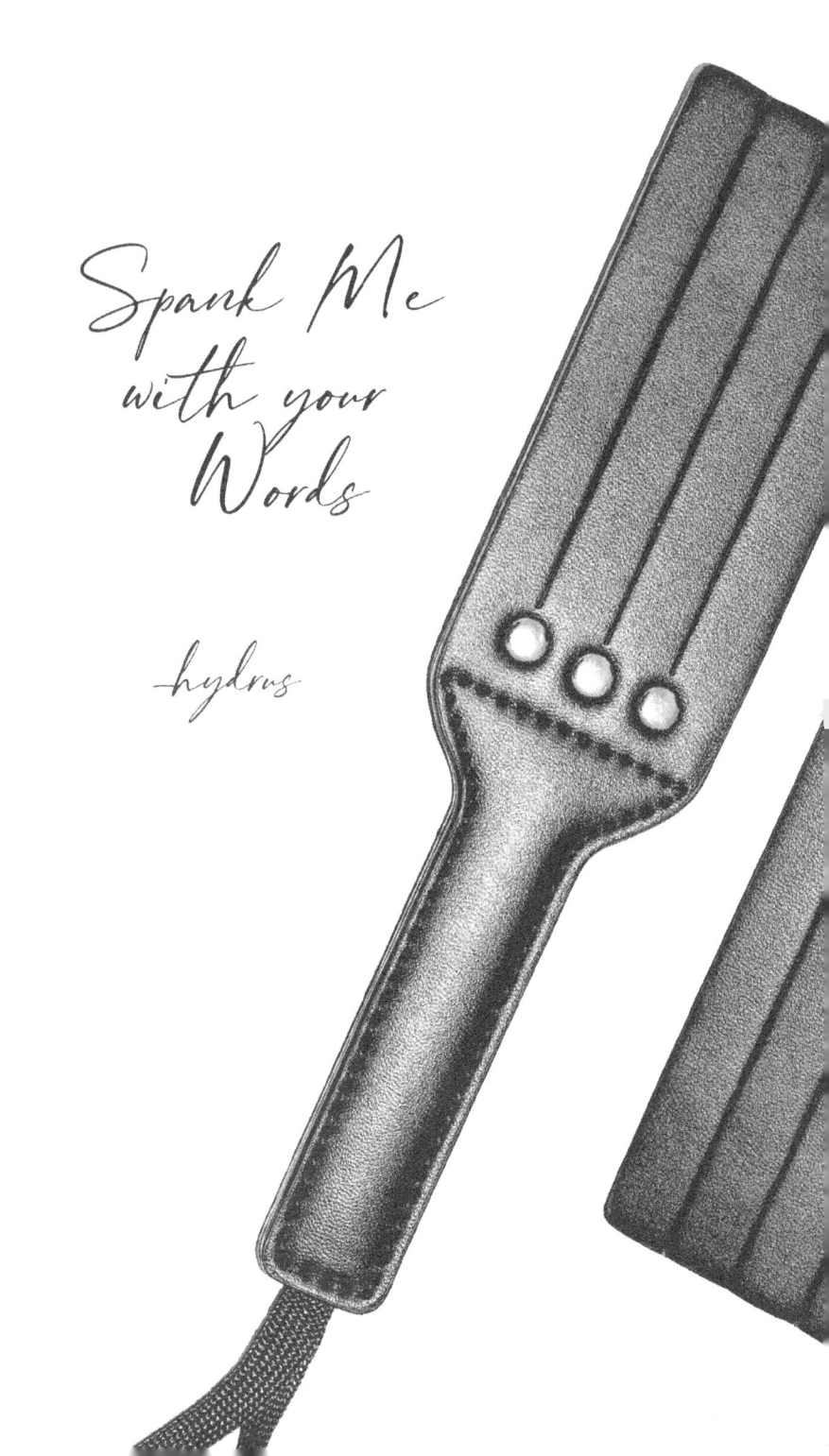

-hydrus

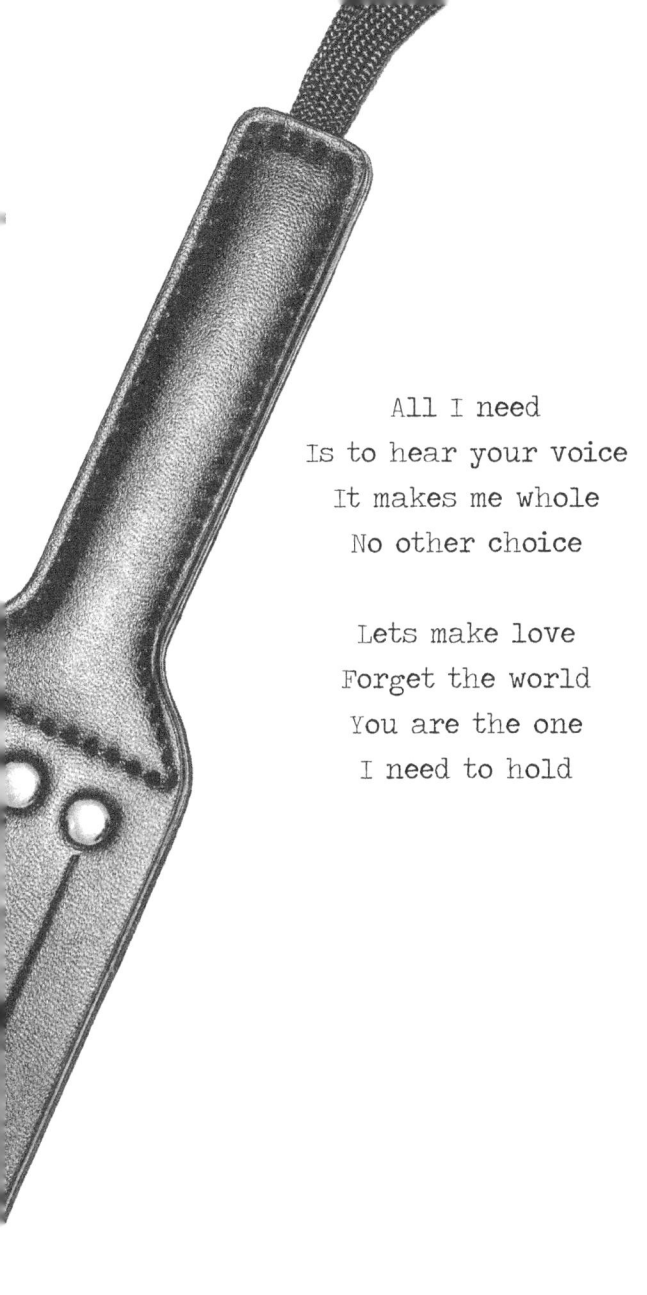

All I need
Is to hear your voice
It makes me whole
No other choice

Lets make love
Forget the world
You are the one
I need to hold

Home
_hydrus

Feel w

you made me do again   hydrus

Slowly twist
Every curve
Feel my weight
My whispered words

On your hips
I mark to claim
Trace my sips
I bend to tame

Blend
_hydrus

Here at home
Is where I wait
No clothes on
In a state

Time just ticks
As I prepare
Your arrival
You unaware

Wanting you
All day long
Craving us
Lust is strong

Hardened muscles
Tense the touch
Gripping length
Missing you so much

Longing
_hydrus

Tightly gripped
Held so firm
Pressing on me
Clothes are torn

Kissing lips
Devouring lust
In your arms
I solely trust

Safe
_hydrus

Dress my chest
With your hair
Grind my soul
Ride me bare

Take my reigns
Grip the beast
Feel it beat
Inside your heat

Melt
_hydrus

Darkened room
Engulfs my night
Hidden hands
Searching in spite

An eager want
As I wait to feel
Probing fingers
Trying to unseal

Starving cravings
The erotic needs
Savage longing
That divulge my greed

Swollen hardness
Twitching in place
Painting you
Leaving my trace

Marked
_hydrus

Fuck I love your body
The way you fit
Between my legs
Eyes that direct
My movements
A tongue that always begs
Never ending hunger
You drip before I feast
Sucking on my fingers
Throbbing just to eat
Never ending passion
Devoured not discreet
Living to consume you
Buried in your heat

Swallowed
_hydrus

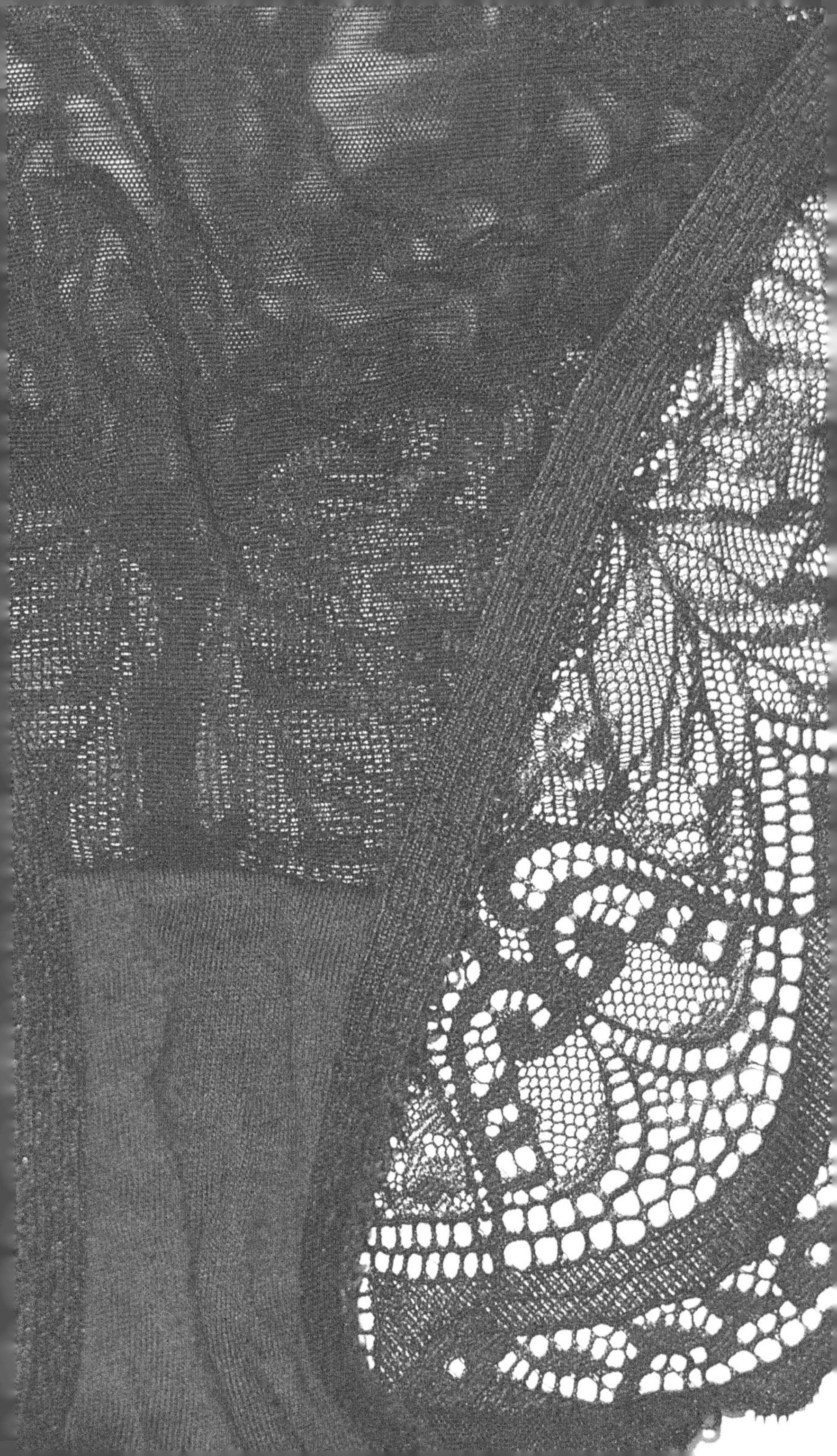

*Your scent
Is why I live*

hydrus

Streaks of sin
Paint her face
Blackened leather
Fiery lace

Steel and chain
Adorn her cage
Pain to play
Embedded rage

Deceptive huntress
Teasing ways
Seduced Temptation
Born to slay

Fearless
_hydrus

At a glance I see
Peering back at me
Skin that is pleased
As kisses tease

Upon my flesh
Is inked your stamp
A lasting mark
Where teeth had clamped

Yours
_hydrus

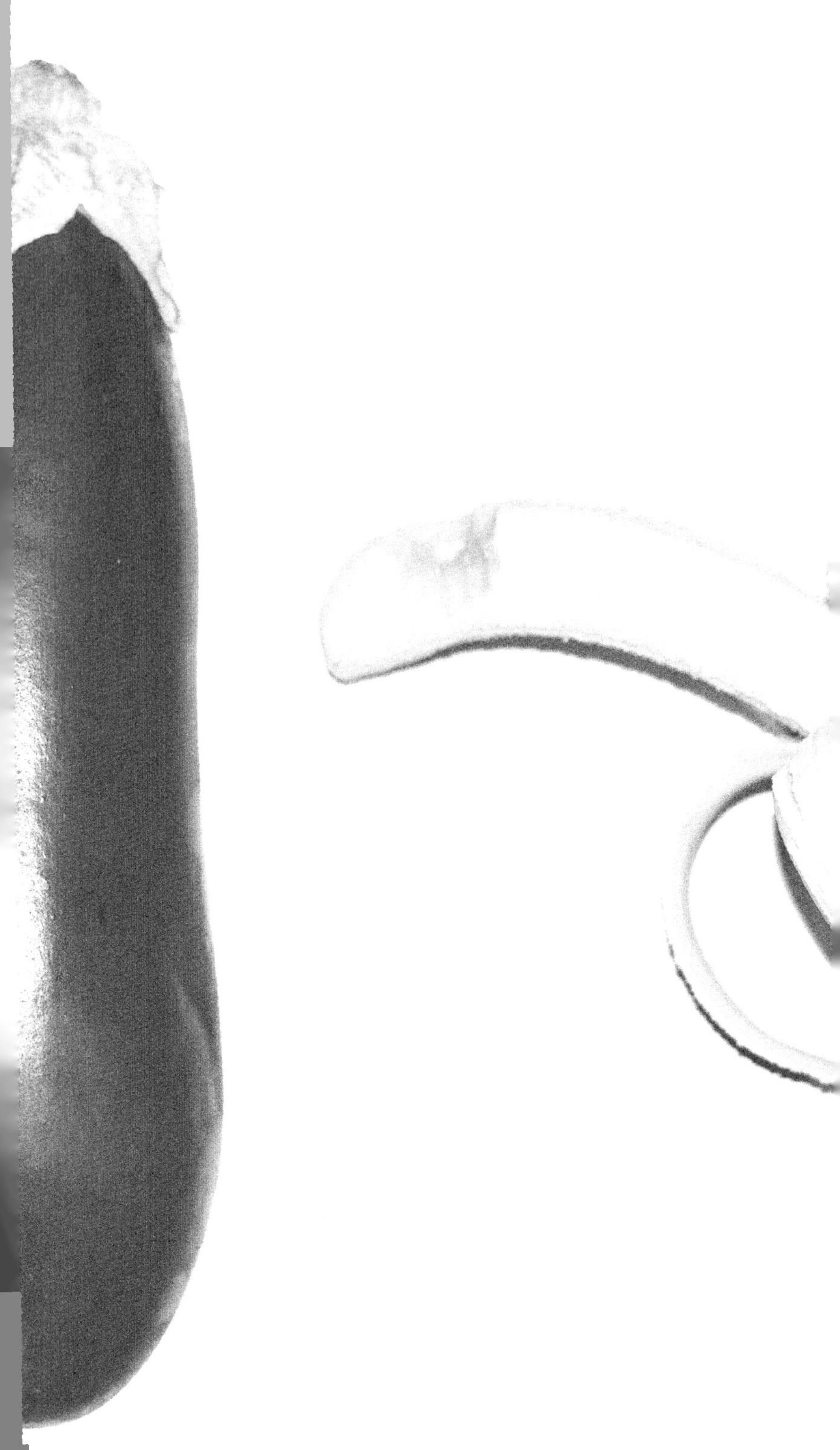

Feel my warmth
As it grows
Heartbeats race
Veins overflow

Slowly throbbing
Stretching skin
Gripping moans
From within

Let it fill
For your taste
Not one drop
Must you waste

In your homes
I will dine
You will drink
All thats mine

Filled
_hydrus

Shady blue eyes glaring
Hidden by silk and sheet
Warm soft skin is moving
Reaching for flesh beneath

Pouty lips upon me
Tracing every hard inch
Bodies moving tightly
Fingers grabbing pinch

Piercing and thrusting heat
Arched and twisted desire
Twisted souls cannot breathe
Quenching ones inner fire

Morning
_hydrus

Hands stand still
Shadows loom
Melted ice sits
A dusty room

Moans are written
Wax has burned
Flesh once bitten
All marks earned

Bodies drenched
Hardened might
Twitching lips
Grips are tight

Heaven sleeps
Hearts still pound
Hunger reaps
Another round

Invitation
_hydrus

Bathed in your scent
I quickly seduce
Open you wide
Quench on your juice

Hands buried in flesh
Tongues trace every line
Consumed in our passion
In your taste
I must dine

Greeting
_hydrus

Savage the stare
That tempts my heart
Yearning a touch
A kiss to start

One touch to follow
Lips to seal
Wonders imagined
Thirsting so real

Desired
_hydrus

Passion awake
Chains untangle
Owner buried
Cravings ravel

Distant menace
Pains not expired
Untangled webs
Flaming desire

Deprived from joy
Emerged to lust
Drenched in new bliss
From the first thrust

Rapt
_hydrus

Take my tongue
Trap my lips
Tempt my soul
Tie my wrists
Trace my veins
Twirl my feast
Taste my demons
Tame my beast

Turn
_hydrus

Im intoxicated by her laugh
The way we fuck and after that
Its not enough and never will
Our urge to fuck its such a thrill

Us
_hydrus

Shivers kindle
Tempted itch
Lurking fingers
Hidden twitch
Lapping tongue
Tip ignites
Gentle strokes
Sweetened bites
Anxious veins
Fuel to sip
Muscles beat
Painted lips

Rush
_hydrus

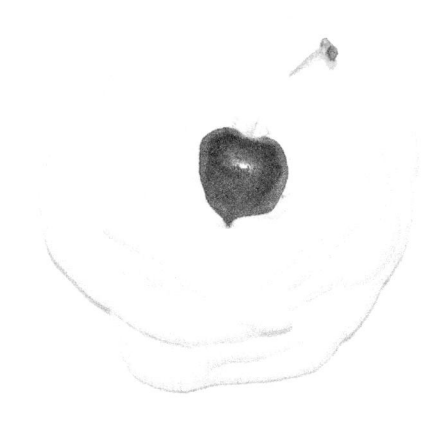

Wear my skin
As I consume your flesh
An appetite
That drips all wet

It never dies
Just lives to feast
Become my meal
Feed your beast

Unchained
_hydrus

A subtle brush
Winks and stare
Little jesters
All unaware

Hinted crush
A stolen smile
Heartbeats rush
So infantile

Guided lessons
Planned attire
Dark exchanges
Both retire

In this hunt
Skin will mix
Prepped desires
With new tricks

Fling
_hydrus

Marks dress our throats
As the broken ropes dance
Red lights hummed
An intoxicated trance

Leather draped walls
Painted on skin
Wet stained lips
Sweat filled sin

Cracking whips kneel
Thick etched air
Eyes remain feeding
Salivating stares

Flavored embers burn
Hungers persist
New pages turn
Only we exist

Impulse
_hydrus

Take your ropes
Tie my wrists
Blindfold my eyes
Enjoy the twist

Belt the flesh
Drain my veins
Lust and lick
Inflict your pain

Enjoy your muse
Your ridden corpse
Extract your ink
Reply your worse

Shattered bat
On a table lay
Reflect in glory
I will have my day

Vow
_hydrus

Taste my lips
They taste of you
Taste our flesh
And all we do

I live for this
And want you to
Taste again
I taste of you

Loops
_hydrus

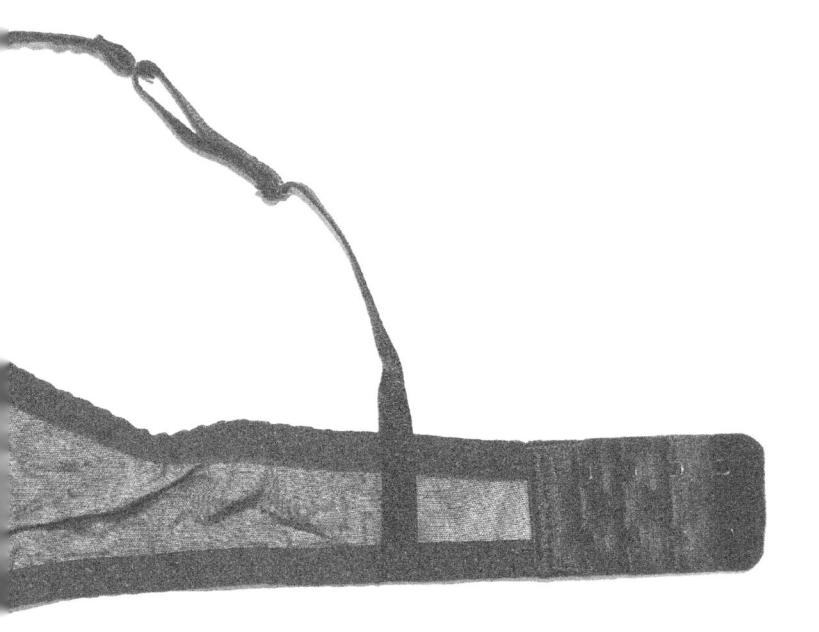

Come closer
Stretch your hand
Under my torso
Stands your man

Take whats yours
Pull with desire
Stroke our passion
Quench your fire

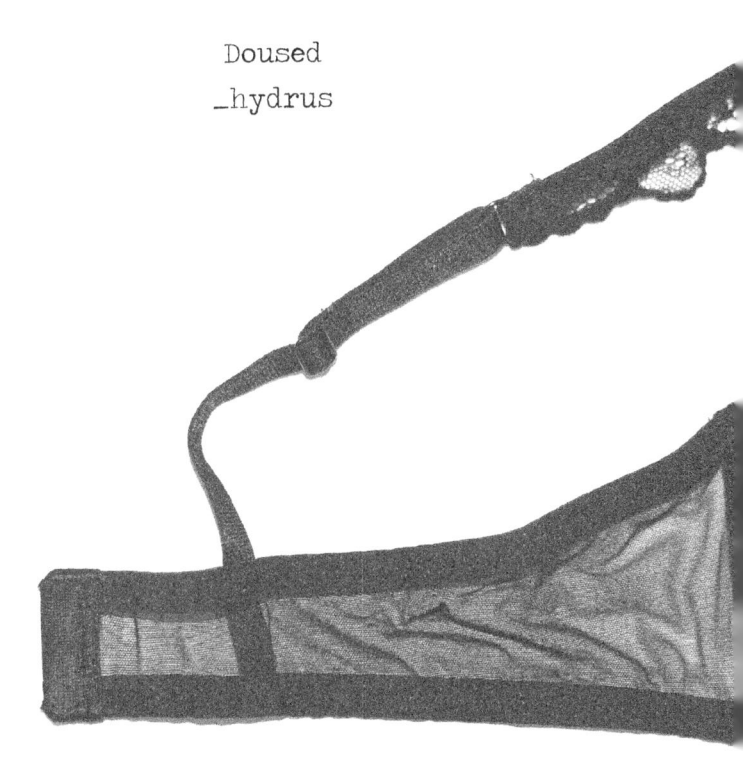

Doused
_hydrus

In the mirror
I can see
All your fingers
Marking me
From my chest
Down to my knees
Ravaged flesh
Waiting to please
Let me mark you
As my own
Show the world
You are not alone
Take me deep
Until you cry
Scream our names
Until we die

Killers
_hydrus

On your knees
We will play
Make them red
As you obey

Pull my leash
Watch you feed
Consume our passion
Pleasure your greed

Daddy
_hydrus

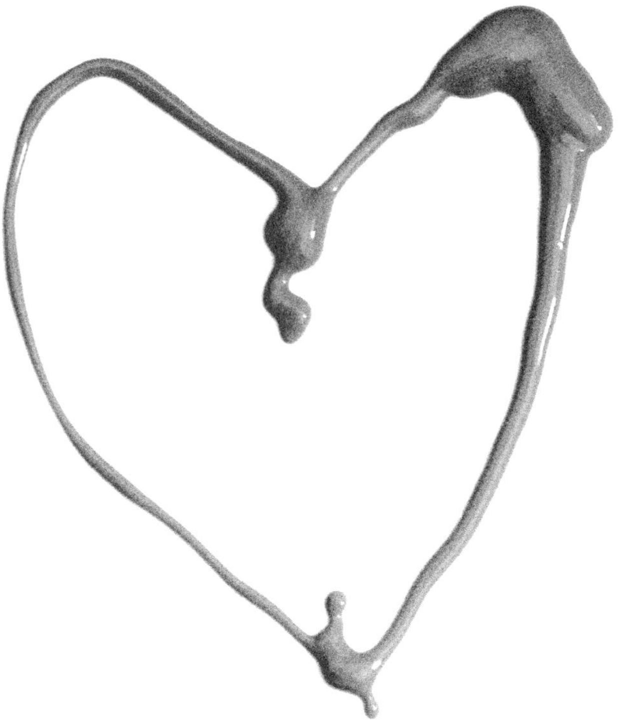

Live to Love

♥ hydrus

Thank

A big and humbled thank you to ALL of YOU
who continue to support and be with me
on this journey.

I am grateful for all of your love and
overwhelming kindness.

To those of you
who have become such bad influences in
my writing and unapologetically kept
encouraging me to write about steamy topics.

And to my trouble Hyde as well.
Who relentlessly hams it up every chance he
gets.

You

To all of my Amazing,
Beautiful and Relentless RAVENS!!
All of you continuously surprise me everyday
with your outpouring generosity and support.
I am so grateful for your kindness and devotion
to me and especially to one another.

Thank you all for being you.

Tysm

To my Sirens.
Cleo, Amina and Elena

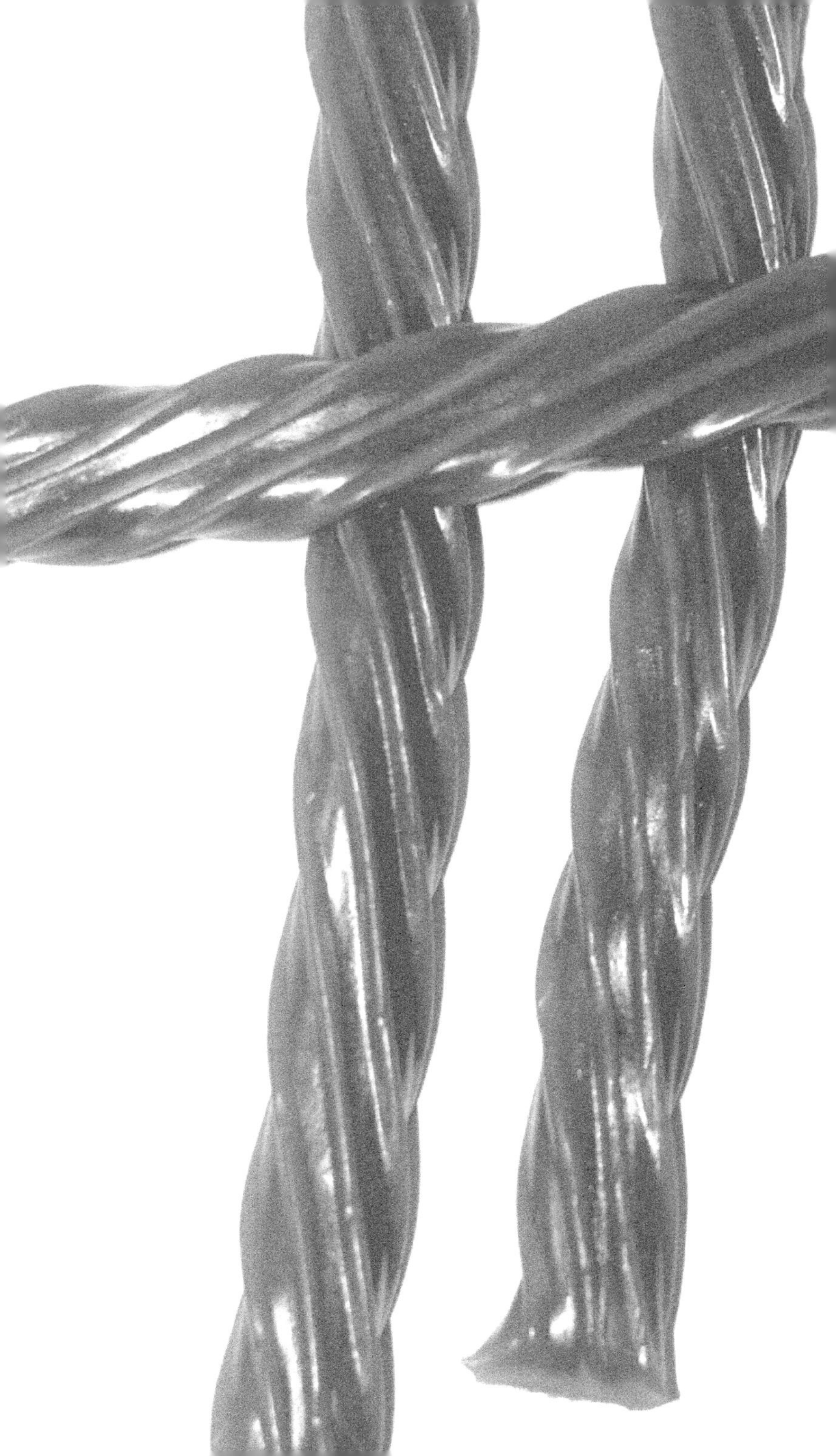

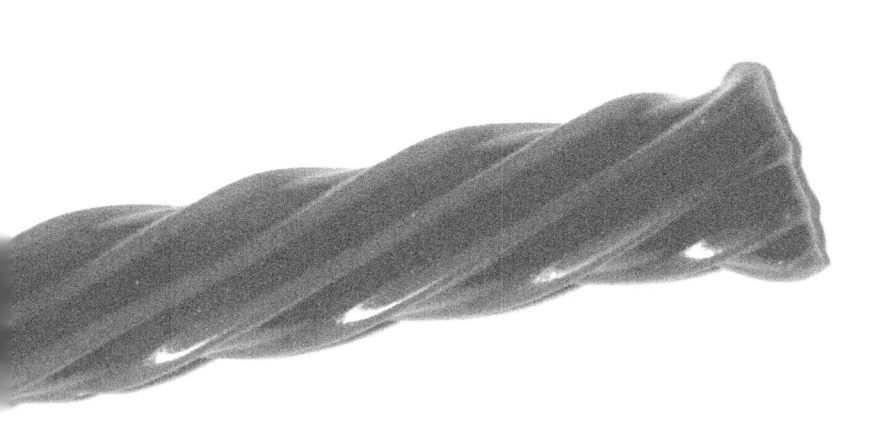

Graze on my lips; and if those hills be dry,
stray lower,
where the pleasant fountains lie.

William Shakespeare

VAL**END**TINE
Playlist

Never Enough	Black Atlass
Love Overdose	Daniel Di Angelo
When We	Tank
Show Me	Black Atlass
Nights	Adrian Daniel
High For This	The Weeknd
Often	The Weeknd
Let's Get Lost	Beck, Bat For Lashes
Pull	Spooky Black
Earned it	The Weeknd
Pillow Talk	Zayn
Love is a Bitch	Two Feet
Falling for You	1975
Use Me	Plaza
Sweat	Zayn
Love from NGC 7318	Tanerelle, Barnes Blvd.
Put It on Me	Matt Maeson
Where you belong	The Weeknd
Two Weeks	FKA twigs
I don't want to Live Forever	Zayn, Taylor Swift
Not Afraid Anymore	Halsey
Bitches Broken Hearts	Billie Eilish
Crazy in Love - Remix	Beyonce
Helium	Sia
Skin	Rihanna
Mine	Bazzi

Listen here:
https://spoti.fi/3uhbuEW

Also by: hydrus

ENDVISIBLE

A collection of poems about the endless feeling of being invisible while going through the emotions and sometimes cruelties of life. Illustrated by the author's own photography, this book guides us through grief, loss and love in a dark and inspiring way typical to how Hydrus's writing helps us cope with reality.

AWAKEND

Tarots cards, much like poems, have the ability to paint a vivid picture of what once was or what could be. They delve into the subtleties that we all carry within ourselves and the secrets that make us who we are.

AwakEND is an immersion into the world of tarot and its mysteries. Read it one way, then another, and let the words guide you into the meaning of each card.
Allow chance and curiosity to accompany you on this incredible journey and let your heart awaken to hope even after having thought everything was lost…

And who knows what secrets you might find out about yourself…

DARK**END**

Is a small look into the world I call my reality.
Through poems, photography and art, I try to capture the ups and downs of this voyage we call life, and sometimes I refer to it as just existing.
Embedded in my words are stories of emotions and feelings that range from the darkest of moments to times of having some type of hope for resolve.

Life is raw and ever-evolving, and we always seem to put ourselves last overall. Time proves to be quite relentless. I hope that we all find common ground through our everyday struggles and in the end, understand that love, although painful at times, can provide so many answers.

So the question then becomes *"how can we better love ourselves?"*

HEART**END**

Is about how we experience love and some of the journeys we embark on when love strikes our heart. It's about the numerous complex phases and ever changing stages of the purest human emotions.
It might be a first kiss, a new romance, a guilty pleasure or a sense of loss but love always helps us reach the heavens or crash down upon its shores.
Love gives even when it takes, it heals and embeds its mark and sculpts us into who we are.

"We all open our hearts and in the end this is the love we bleed."
_hydrus

ENDTHOLOGY

Is a collection of poems drawn up from experiences, thoughts, and emotions. Not everything in the world is dark, but many times we live without any light. We lose ourselves in what we consider our reality. Our souls forget what is important. At the same time, we rejoice when we regain our passion and our inner light.

We might live many lives, but which one will you always remember?

What memories will we ink?

What will have true meaning?

How will we live our END?

_hydrus

ENDLOVE
ENDPAIN

A collection of poems that deal with the human struggle of being in love. The emotional roller coaster and the ups and downs that our souls take on this journey. This path is one of endless bliss but sometimes agony.

Love is always a conflict of raw emotion and trust. It is a journey we seek to take and at times we regret we do. It is a struggle between good vs. evil but mostly in ourselves.

About The Author

Anonymous poet, photographer and artist,
Hydrus documents through his poems the darkness and the
glimmers of life taunting us when we are in the shadows,
as well as many of the little things which make a colossal impact
on who we are.

Connect with hydrus:

Website: www.hydruspoetry.com
Instagram: @hydruspoetry
Facebook: www.facebook.com/hydruspoetry
TikTok: @_hydrusravens
Redbubble Merchandise:
www.redbubble.com/people/hydruspoetry/explore

Everything
About you
Is more than
Sexy...
Its
Intoxicatingly
Wild

♥hydrus

Made in the USA
Monee, IL
09 April 2022